This book is dedicated to anyone who came to the States with a dream and used their work, charisma, and influence to leave America better than when they found it.

Just like my dad. I miss you every minute of every day.

— D.R.

For my family members who came here for a better life. Thank you.

For all those who do the same.

— J.C.

A FEIWEL AND FRIENDS BOOK

An imprint of Macmillan Publishing Group, LLC

120 Broadway, New York, NY 10271

WATCH ME. Text copyright © 2021 by Doyin Richards. Illustrations copyright © 2021 by Joe Cepeda.

All rights reserved. Printed in China by RR Donnelley Asia Printing Solutions Ltd., Dongguan City, Guangdong Province

Our books may be purchased in bulk for promotional, educational, or business use. Please contact your local bookseller or the Macmillan Corporate and Premium Sales Department at (800) 221-7945 ext. 5442 or by email at MacmillanSpecialMarkets@macmillan.com.

Library of Congress Cataloging-in-Publication Data is available.

ISBN 978-1-250-26651-4

Book design by Rich Deas and Kathleen Breitenfeld

Feiwel and Friends logo designed by Filomena Tuosto

First edition, 2021

The artwork was created with oils over acrylic on board.

1 3 5 7 9 10 8 6 4 2

mackids.com

A Story of Immigration and Inspiration

WATCH ME

Doyin Richards

illustrated by Joe Cepeda

FEIWEL AND FRIENDS
NEW YORK

Joe grew up in Sierra Leone, a small West African country.

He had nice manners, got good grades, and, like you, always listened to his parents.

Well, maybe not always.

Joe had goals and dreams, like you.

He knew he had to make a big move in order to achieve them.

Joe wanted to go to America.

His friends and family said people would laugh at his accent and fear his dark skin.

They said he'd never fit in.

He was different. Perhaps like you.
Joe smiled and said, "Watch me."

His friends and family were right.

The food in America was strange.
The music was new, and, perhaps like you, he enjoyed it.

But Joe still missed Sierra Leone.

In America, some people teased Joe about his accent and dark skin.
Some people told him to go back to Africa.

It hurt Joe to be hated for things he couldn't control.
Just like it hurts you. Maybe going back home to Africa
was the safe and easy thing to do.

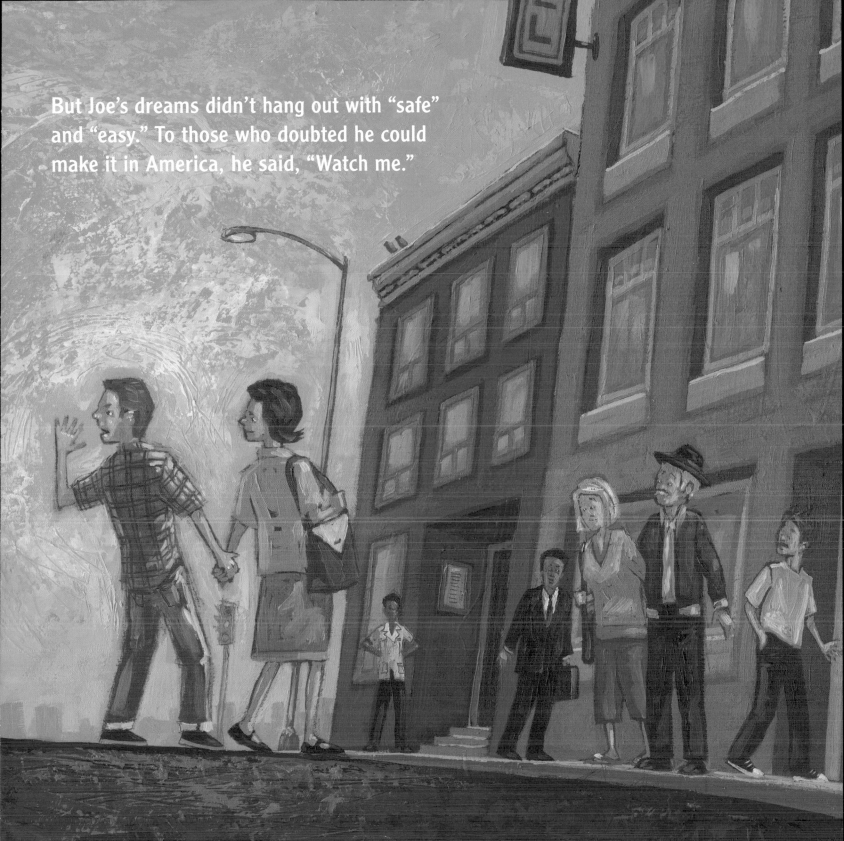

But Joe's dreams didn't hang out with "safe" and "easy." To those who doubted he could make it in America, he said, "Watch me."

Look around. Do you see people like Joe?

Do you watch them learn and study, surrounded by books?

Do you watch them as they deal
with all kinds of looks?

Do you watch them throw an awesome curveball?

Do you watch them eat lunch by themselves down the hall?

They come by plane. Perhaps like you.
They come by boat. Maybe you did, too.

Watch them. See them.

This land is your land. This land is our land.
There is enough for everyone.

But what about Joe?

Joe studied and, perhaps like you, he studied hard.
He knew he had to work twice as hard at school
to prove that he actually belonged there.

Many of his teachers and classmates thought he wouldn't graduate.

"Watch me," Joe said.

And at the end of his school years, he was Dr. Joe.

How do I know?

Because Dr. Joe was my dad.

Right now, a kid is dreaming of coming to America to become the next Dr. Joe.

You don't think she can do it?

"Watch me," she says, and smiles.